MW01070563

Written by

Killian Wolf

Published in association with
Bear With Us Productions

© 2022 Killian Wolf
Little Krampus and the Mischievous Yule Lads

The right of Killian Wolf as the author of
this work has been asserted by her in
accordance with the Copyright Designs
and Patents Act 1988.
All rights reserved, including the right of
reproduction in whole or part in any form.

Paperback ISBN: 978-1-951140-12-0
Hardback ISBN: 978-1-951140-13-7

Cover by Richie Evans
Design by Luisa Moschetti
Illustrated by Alice Pieroni
Edited by: The Stardust Experience

killianwolf.com
www.justbearwithus.com

Illustrated by
Alice Pieroni

Written by
Killian Wolf

A cold, wintry wind whipped around with a moan,
But one little Krampus was warm in his home.
At snuggling on sofas young Klaus was no rookie,
Slurping his cocoa and crunching on cookies.

Slouched on the couch, his pink nose sniffed the air,
The fresh scent of gingerbread swirled everywhere.
Slurp, munch, sniff, crunch! went the satisfied child,
When Mother saw Klaus on the couch, she just smiled.

His mother had finished mixing a chocolate fruit cake,
She sat beside Dad, waiting for it to bake.

"Mother," said Klaus, "would it be a real pain,
To tell me the tale of the Yule Lads again?"
"Yes!" replied Father. "Now you must pipe down.
They'll hear you and come when we're not around."

Mother just chuckled. "It's worth telling twice,
The tale of the lads from the land full of ice."
She grabbed the last cookie. "Those Yule Lads are rude,
They come to bring terror and take all your food."
"And keep your eyes peeled, Klaus," started Father, "for soon,
They'll swipe all your socks and they'll steal all your spoons."

"What if they are here?" asked Klaus, his eyes wide,
His fur standing on end. "Will we have time to hide?"
The whole house was warm, but Klaus started to quiver,
"Or sh-should we run?" he asked Dad with a shiver.

"There's no need," Mom said with a smile, with a nod to the fire,
"While *that* log stays lit, those Yule Lads will retire.
They will come one by one, not two by two,
And always stay away if that log burns the night through."

"So *don't* blow it out,"
Father said with a frown,
"And help keep the cold out,
pull the shades down!"

"Okay," said Klaus, staring into the fire,
He held his breath, hoping the flames didn't expire.
"What *if* it goes out and the Yule Lads get in?"
"Then **POOF!**" yelled Dad—Klaus nearly jumped out his skin!
"Light the log." Father laughed "And they'll go **POP!**"

"Enough," Mother said, "now this shouting must stop.

The best way to make the lads listen to you,
Is saying their names one by one, like I do."
The big Yule log **crackled**, all wrapped up in flame.
Little Klaus giggled. "Please! Tell me their names!"
The old tale was scary, but Klaus was excited,
For his favorite part, which his mother recited.

"There's Sheep-Cote and Gully-Gawk, followed by Stubby,
You'll know the last fellow, since he's so short and chubby.
Spoon-Licker, Pot-Scraper, Bowl-Licker too,
I *wouldn't* leave our leftovers out now, would you?

Door-Slammer, Skyr-Gobbler, and Sausage-Swiper,
The first one will wake you up, he's a real griper.
Next, Window-Peeper and Door-Sniffer come,
Looking to steal things or hunting breadcrumbs.

Then you'll meet Meat-Hook, and last, Candle-Beggar,
He'll nick all our wicks and then creep off forever."

When the list finished, Klaus giggled again,
"Thanks Mother, **I think they're such funny names!**"

The big Yule log *flickered* with flames in the fire,
As Mother continued, Klaus felt a bit tired.

"In old times, when Santa was known as Saint Nick,
Lived thirteen young brothers who **loved** to play tricks.
Half-troll and half-ogre, they kept themselves hidden,
High on a mountain that soon was forbidden.

And just before Christmas, they'd climb down their hill,
To steal and play pranks on the people at will.

Young Klaus was so cozy, bathed in the warm light,
He couldn't keep his eyes open, try as he might.
"Bedtime," said Father, "those eyelids look heavy."

As Dad picked him up, Klaus complained, "I'm not ready!
The story's not done, I could stay up 'til dawn,
I *just* want to hear . . ." said Klaus, *yawn, yawn, yawn, yawn!*

A little while later, Klaus woke up in bed.
"Did I hear a noise? Or was it in my head?"
He sat up to listen and all-round the house,
No creature was stirring, not even a . . .
CRASH!

Terrified, Klaus felt his teeth start to chatter,
He wondered just **what** could be causing that clatter.
"It can't be Santa," he thought, "that's not right,
There's still thirteen days 'til his sleigh flies all night."
Klaus put his hooves on the hard wooden floor,

And crept from his bedroom
to find out for sure.

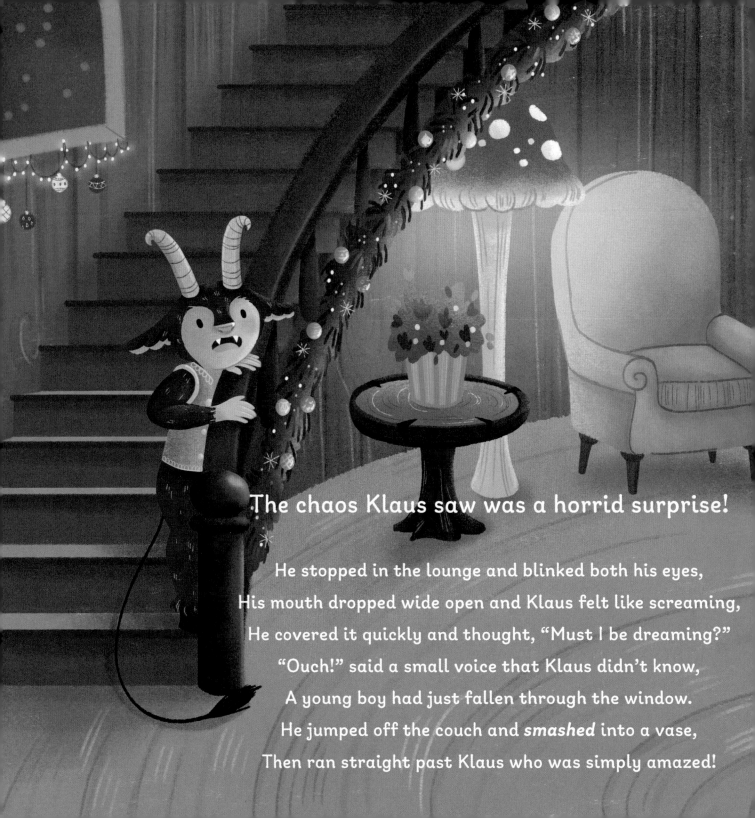

The chaos Klaus saw was a horrid surprise!

He stopped in the lounge and blinked both his eyes,
His mouth dropped wide open and Klaus felt like screaming,
He covered it quickly and thought, "Must I be dreaming?"
"Ouch!" said a small voice that Klaus didn't know,
A young boy had just fallen through the window.
He jumped off the couch and *smashed* into a vase,
Then ran straight past Klaus who was simply amazed!

The boy had long ears and a pointy big nose,
"Was that Window-Peeper?" asked Klaus. "I suppose!"

Boing! Two boys bounced on the couch without fear,
"WHEEE!" cried one, swinging on Mom's chandelier.
"Stop!" shouted Klaus. "Tell me, who are you all?"
The boys simply laughed and ran into the hall.
The question was answered when Klaus saw their features,
He knew they were half-troll and half-ogre creatures.
"They *must* be the Yule Lads," said Klaus. "I've no doubt."
And that's when he saw that the fire had gone out.

"But *who* put it out?" wondered Klaus with a frown,
The cold must have blown in—that window's not down!
"Uh-oh," he realized, "that was my task,
But I got distracted as soon as Dad asked."

Little Klaus gulped a big lump in his throat,
"I must prove I'm worthy of my furry coat,
Though facing those creatures fills me with distress,
It's up to *me* now to fix my own mess."

But in the kitchen the mess was much worse,
Horrified, Klaus didn't know *where* to look first,
Gulp! went a Yule Lad while dancing a jig,
Swigging down milk by the wide-open fridge.
Another lad helped him by pouring it out,
And scooped the froth from the pail into his mouth.
His fist full of yogurt, Skyr-Gobbler just beamed,
The greedy lad looked like a cat with the cream.
"Hey! That is *our* milk!" said Klaus with a wail,
The bad lads didn't stop. They were beyond the pale!

BANG! By the stove was a lad with a pan,
Striking it with a knife, making a *CLANG!*
"You'll wake up my parents," Klaus said in fright,
"Don't you know not to be noisy at night?"
Slurp! went a Yule Lad who looked very lean,
He juggled with spoons while he licked them all clean.

Nearby, a boy stuck his head in the sink,
He scraped all the plates and looked tickled pink.
"Those are **mom's** spoons," called Klaus. "That's just rude.
Stop eating that sausage. You're stealing our food!"
The kitchen was almost cleaned out by the strangers,

Klaus **panicked.**
He knew what would next be in danger.

Crossing the kitchen on his cloven feet,
Klaus saw on the counter Mom's freshly baked treat.
And standing right there with a grin of delight,

A Yule Lad was ready to take a big bite.

Would Klaus be in time to fix his big mistake,
And stop this bad Yule Lad from taking the cake?

Klaus grabbed the cake with a second to spare,

The greedy lad took a big bite of fresh air.

Klaus staggered backward and tried to stay steady,

"This cake full of fruit is surprisingly heavy!"

He teetered and toppled and stumbled some more,

And fell in slow **mo-oh-tion** onto the floor.

"The cake is okay." He sighed. "What a relief!"

He put it high on a shelf, far from the thief.
Now worried Klaus hurried back to the fridge,
The milky-faced lad was still dancing his jig.
"Leave it," said Klaus as he closed the fridge door,
"Next I must get those spoons back in the drawer."
But *just* as he felt things were going to plan,
Klaus almost jumped out of his skin once again. **SLAM!**

The noise was so loud that it rattled the house,
This night surely *hadn't* been as quiet as a mouse.
Klaus peeked round the corner and saw his worst fear,

The loudest of all the Yule Lads had appeared!
His hand on the handle, this lad was to blame,
He shut the door over and over again.

Door-Slammer smiled and he looked strangely sweet,
Then **STOMPED** even louder with both of his feet.

The crisis was growing.
Klaus fell to his knees,

"Please stop all this stomping, I'm begging you please!
I'll get coal for Christmas if you wake up my dad,
I didn't close that window. He's going to be mad!
We'll *all* get in trouble, it won't just be me,
There'll only be coal below *your* Christmas tree."

Ping! Like a lightbulb over his head,
Klaus had an idea. "What was it Mom said?

They'll listen if I say their names one by one,
They'll help me clear up, then the lads will be gone.

There's still a chance that I can fix my mistake,
And tidy this mess before Mom and Dad wake."
But just as Klaus tried to remember Mom's list,
His chance to clean up had already been missed.

"KLAUS!"

shouted Father, which boomed through the hall,
"*What* has been going on here? Who are all—"
Dad stopped mid-sentence. The sight was so shocking

"I can explain,"

said Klaus, whose knees were knocking.

"A cold wintry wind must have blown the fire out,
I didn't close the window, it's my fault, don't shout."
Dad *thumped* his hooves down the hall, like a speeding rocket,
Passing a Yule Lad with candle-stuffed pockets.
Dad stopped by the kitchen and quietly fumed,
Hands on his horns at the state of the room.

Soon Mom had joined him there, dragged out of bed,
To this kitchen nightmare, her hands on her head.
"Is this true?" Mother asked. "Am I awake?"
"I'm *sorry*." Klaus sighed. "But I did save your cake."

"Leave this to me," Father said with a frown,
He walked to the fireplace—the Yule Lads calmed down.
As soon as the boys heard him lighting a match,
They all knew the plan Father Krampus had hatched.

Strike! In the kitchen, the spoon-licking stopped,
No swigging of milk, or scraping of pots.

Strike! In the hallway the stomping died out,
The house was quiet all throughout.

Strike! All the Yule Lads were frozen with fear,
Would Dad light the log and make them disappear?

Suddenly, little Klaus had a surprise,
He saw something in the boys' wide, frightened eyes.

**"What if they came here for warmth and for food?
They're playful—what if they didn't *mean* to be rude?"**

When Klaus looked again at the Yule Lads, all scared,
He knew that they just needed someone who cared.

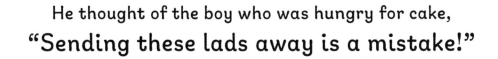

He thought of the boy who was hungry for cake,
"Sending these lads away is a mistake!"

"WAIT!" shouted Klaus. It was Dad's turn to jump.
He **whacked** his head on the lamp, raising a bump.
"What is it *now*?" Father asked with a glare.
"Don't light the log!" Klaus cried. "It wouldn't be fair!
I don't want to watch all these Yule Lads go *poof*,
I think we should welcome them under our roof.
They might be unruly, but they can be saved,
If I make them listen, they *might* just behave."

Klaus **gulped**, hoping he would get all the names right,
He looked at the lads and began to recite.

"There's Sheep-Cote and Gully-Gawk, followed by Stubby,
Now that I've met him, he isn't that chubby.

Spoon-Licker, Pot-Scraper, Bowl-Licker too,
You did all the dishes, that's most kind of you.

Door-Slammer, Skyr-Gobbler, and Sausage-Swiper,
You did so much stomping I thought you were hyper.

Next, Window-Peeper and Door-Sniffer came,
But I left it open so you weren't to blame.

Then I met Meat-Hook and last, Candle-Beggar,

**I've said all your names now,
so gather together."**

Thirteen small, hungry mouths dropped in surprise,
Klaus now had fixed on him twenty-six eyes.
Glad that the log hadn't gone up in flames,
Gully-Gawk asked, "How do *you* know our names?"
"Never mind that," said Klaus, "I have a treat.

Would anyone here like
something to eat?"

As thirteen small hands were stuck high in the air,

Klaus ran to the kitchen for something to share.

On the high shelf was his Mom's freshly baked,

Chocolatey, fruit-filled (and quite heavy) cake.

The Yule Lads had followed Klaus like the Pied Piper,
"That looks **delicious**, Klaus!" said a drooling Sausage-Swiper.
They followed him out like the kids in the fable,
And Klaus placed the cake on the dining room table.
"I want to share this cake with you lads," said a smiling Klaus.
"*Mmm mmm mmm mmm!*" replied thirteen full mouths.
Then Mother Krampus came in. "Klaus is right,
It's **great** to see all of you smile with delight.

Everyone needs love, affection, and laughter,

Now let's see if I have the things you were after."

Clang! went the saucepans that Mom passed around,

As well as the sausages Father had found,

Clink! went the spoons that Klaus gave to the lickers,

While milk from the pail was gulped down even quicker.

Cheer! went Skyr-Gobbler who had a big grin,

As thick, creamy yogurt drooled all down his chin.

Soon, the thirteen Yule Lads had all they desired,
For full hearts and bellies were all they required.

"Thanks," said Door-Sniffer, "for sharing your home,
Because of your kindness we feel less alone."
The lad turned to Dad. "And I *know* that we stole,
So thanks for not giving us big lumps of coal."

Father and Mother hugged Klaus very tight,
"We're proud of you," Mom said, "for doing what's right."
"Yes." Father nodded. "Most others would fail,
To share with these boys when they'd heard the old tales."

Little Klaus *gulped* and to his big surprise,
He realized that tears of joy filled up his eyes.
Klaus looked at Dad who he really admired,
He still felt so bad that he'd blown out the fire.

"You're not mad at me then, Dad? I thought you were."
"Of *course* I'm not." Father laughed, ruffling his fur.
**"It's just a mistake, that's all, no need to weep,
Besides, my boy, I also fell fast asleep!"**

That night they played games with the mischievous lads,
With cookies and cake that made everyone glad.
Half-ogre, half-troll, but now firm family friends,
The Yule Lads brought laughter that never would end.

And later, when little Klaus crept to his bed,
As *yawn* after *yawn* after yawn left his head,
He found on his pillow a hand-scribbled note,
"It's from a Yule Lad! Let's see what they wrote."

We like to make mischief and play lots of pranks,
But it's not a trick when we give you our thanks.
We've never been given a present before,
But your kindness must be the best one for sure.
That night in December we'll always hold dear,
Thirteen days before Christmas: the best of the year.
P.S. One last thing, Klaus, and please don't be shocked.
You might find we've taken all your left socks.

About the Author

 There are two things in the world Killian Wolf enjoys doing: writing and reading stories about folklore.

When she's not doing those things, you might find her following fairies to far away lands or playing hide-and-seek with dragons.
Killian also writes Urban Fantasy novels and lives in England with her husband and her tornado of a cat, Oliver.

She hopes you enjoy reading her fairytales as much as she loves writing them. To find out about her books and magical worlds, visit her at **killianwolf.com.**

IG: @killian_wolf_storybooks
FB: @killianwolfstorybooks
website: killianwolf.com

Now Available!

Don't forget to join Little Krampus in
**Little Krampus and The Magical Sleigh Ride and
Little Krampus and the Christmas Secret!**

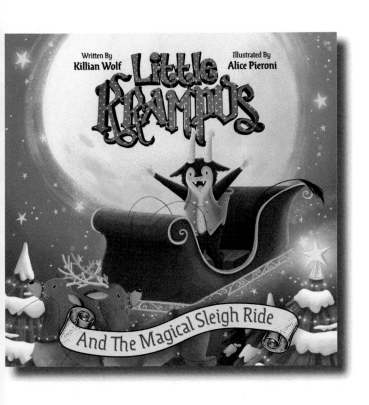

The Company

Bear With Us Productions is a company dedicated to illustrating and developing high-quality children's books for new and existing authors all over the world. The company is known for its friendly attitude and professional work ethic which has made them the 'go-to guys,' for high-quality children's book development, predominantly within the self-publishing sector.

Bear With Us Productions employs over 60 children's book illustrators and professional designers from a multitude of places around the world and loves dealing with the rich diversity in illustration styles that this brings to the numerous projects the company develops.

justbearwithus.com
FB: @bearwithusproductions
IG: bear_with_us_productions

The Illustrator

Alice Pieroni was born in Fano, Italy in 1991.
She graduated with a degree in illustration from the "International School of Comics," and started illustrating children's books because she has always wanted to make children happy through her drawings.
Her style is constantly evolving, and every day she strives to improve herself, preferring colours that recall traditional ones, such as watercolours and pencils.

She collaborated with Bear With Us Production for the books "Little Krampus and the Magical Sleigh Ride," "Santa Goes Sledding on Christmas Eve," and "Little Krampus and the Christmas Secret."
She also worked with some publishing houses in recent years including Dami Editori, Editions Grenouille, Auggie Bear Publishing, Little Lamb Books, and Gribaudo Edizioni.

Made in the USA
Middletown, DE
04 December 2022

16967813R00027